The Case of the Two Masked Robbers

An I Can Read Book®

The Case of the Two Masked Robbers

story and pictures by

Lillian Hoban

HarperTrophy

A Division of HarperCollins*Publishers*

The Case of the Two Masked Robbers
Copyright © 1986 by Lillian Hoban
Printed in the U.S.A. All rights reserved.
First Harper Trophy edition, 1988.

Library of Congress Cataloging-in-Publication Data
Hoban, Lillian.
    The case of the two masked robbers.

    (An I can read book)
    Summary: Raccoon twins Arabella and Albert track
down the robbers who stole Mrs. Turtle's eggs.
    [1. Raccoons—Fiction.   2. Twins—Fiction.
3. Animals—Fiction.   4. Mystery and detective stories]
I. Title.   II. Title: Case of the 2 masked robbers.
III. Series.
PZ7.H635Cas   1986   [E]   85-45819
ISBN 0-06-022298-0
ISBN 0-06-022299-9 (lib. bdg.)

    "A Harper Trophy book"
ISBN 0-06-444121-0 (pbk.)

For Esmé

One evening

Grandpa Raccoon hurried

to Arabella and Albert's house.

"There has been a holdup,"

he called.

"Where?" asked the twins.

"At Meadow Marsh Bank,"
said Grandpa.

"Two robbers stole the eggs
that Mrs. Turtle deposited."

"Did the cops catch the robbers?"

asked Arabella.

"Will there be a shoot-out?"

asked Albert.

"Were there any clues?"

asked Mr. Raccoon.

"No," said Grandpa.

"The robbers wore masks

and long, dark coats.

They moved slowly.

They were very scary.

After the robbery,

one went east

and one went west.

Nobody dared to follow them."

"I bet I could find more clues,"

said Arabella.

"Me too!" said Albert.

"I would catch those robbers fast!"

The twins went to bed.

They could not fall asleep.

"I wonder who stole those eggs,"
whispered Albert.

"I bet we can solve the mystery,"
said Arabella.

The twins lay awake a long time.

Suddenly,

Arabella said,

"Albert, *we* have masks.

All we need are long, dark coats.

Then we will look like the robbers."

Arabella tiptoed to the closet.

She came back

with two big, dark coats.

"Here," she said to Albert.

"Put this on and let's go!"

"Where are we going?" asked Albert.

"We are going to find the robbers,"

said Arabella.

"Robbers are dangerous," said Albert.

"Not if they think

we are robbers!"

said Arabella.

The twins tiptoed past the kitchen.

They slipped quietly

out the front door.

They ran through the shadowy woods.

An owl hooted,

"Twoo-hoo! Twoo-hoo!"

"Arabella," Albert whispered.

"Maybe the real robbers

are hiding near here."

"I hope so," said Arabella.

"Grandpa said

one robber went east

and one robber went west.

Now it is dark.

They will meet back here.

They will split up the loot,

and we will be there to catch them!"

The twins came

to the edge of the woods.

There was Meadow Marsh Bank.

"I think the robbers will meet here,"

whispered Arabella.

"Sshh!" said Albert.

"I hear something!"

Arabella and Albert sat very still.

They could hear the wind

in the leaves.

They could hear the birds

peeping softly in the trees.

They could hear

a swish-swish-swishing.

It came closer

and closer

AND

CLOSER.

"It is one of the robbers!"

whispered Arabella.

"It is moving slowly,

just like Grandpa said!"

"It is a snake!" yelled Albert.

"I am getting out of here!"

Albert jumped into the bushes.

23

The snake slithered

over a root.

It stopped in front of Arabella.

Arabella saw the snake's tongue
dart in and out.

She was afraid to move.

"Where is your hump?"

hissed the snake.

"What hump?" asked Arabella.

"The hump on your back,"

hissed the snake.

"You had a hump

when you stole Mrs. Turtle's eggs.

You are wearing

the same coat and mask.

But now you do not have a hump."

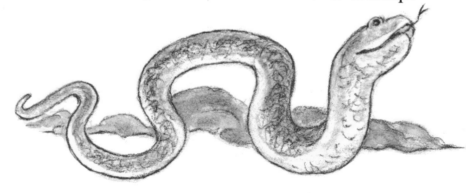

"I am not a robber," said Arabella.

"My brother and I

are looking for the robbers.

We want to scare them.

Then they will give back the eggs."

"I just saw your brother,"

said the snake.

"He *was* moving much faster

than the robbers!"

The snake slithered

out of sight.

"Albert," called Arabella softly.

"The snake is gone."

Albert did not answer.

Suddenly,

there were hoarse squawks

near Meadow Marsh Bank.

"HELP! HELP! LET ME GO!"

yelled Albert.

"Oh!" cried Arabella.

"The robbers have Albert!"

She ran quickly

to Meadow Marsh Bank.

She saw two dark, shadowy figures.

They were holding Albert

upside down.

They were shaking him.

"AAAWK! AAAWK!

ROBBER! ROBBER! ROBBER!"

they croaked.

33

"I am not a robber!"

yelled Albert.

"Put me down, you old crows!"

"Give us the eggs!"

croaked one of the crows.

"YUM! YUM!"

croaked the other crow.

"Scrambled eggs, poached eggs,

fried eggs!

GIVE BACK

THOSE LOVELY TURTLE EGGS!"

The crows shook Albert

until his teeth chattered.

Arabella stepped forward.

"REACH FOR THE SKY, CROWS!"

she yelled.

"I HAVE YOU COVERED!"

"YAAAWK! YAAAWK!"

screeched the crows.

"HELP! ANOTHER ROBBER!"

"We are not robbers,"

said Arabella.

"We thought *you* were the robbers."

"We are not robbers,"

said one of the crows.

"We flew over to eat...oops...

I mean...to see

Mrs. Turtle's eggs.

We eat...I mean...see

her eggs every year.

When we got here,

the eggs were gone!"

"Sneaky Mrs. Turtle,"

said the other crow.

"She always deposited her eggs

at Duckweed Swamp Bank before."

"Well," said Arabella.

"I am glad the eggs were stolen

before you got here.

You are very nasty

to eat them every year."

"If that is the way you feel,

we will leave right now,"

said the crows.

"We have seen a snake,"

said Albert.

"We have seen some crows.

But we have not seen the robbers."

"The snake and the crows

gave us two more clues!"

said Arabella.

"Come on, let's go!"

"Wait a minute," said Albert.

"I know all the other clues.

But what is the snake's clue?"

Arabella whispered in Albert's ear.

"You are right," said Albert.

"The snake gave us a great clue!"

The twins ran through the woods
to their house.

"Let's leave our coats on the porch,"
whispered Arabella.

"We do not want to look like robbers."

Then they slipped away

to the other side of the pond.

They found the old log house

by the light of the moon.

Arabella knocked at the door.

"Who is there?" called a voice.

"It is the Raccoon twins,"
said Albert.

"We know who stole the eggs."

"Go away," said another voice.

"We have had enough trouble."

"Please let us in,"

said Arabella.

"We came to help."

The door opened a crack.

Mr. Turtle stuck out his head.

"Come in," he said.

Mrs. Turtle was sitting

at the kitchen table.

On the table was a basket.

In the basket

were the stolen TURTLE EGGS!

"We knew the eggs

would be here," said Albert.

"How did you know that?"

asked Mrs. Turtle.

"Well," said Arabella.

"We knew that the robbers ran slowly.

Turtles run very slowly.

We knew that the robbers

had humps on their backs.

Turtles have shells.

The shells would look like humps

under long coats."

"That's right," said Albert.

"Then we found the crows.

They were looking for the eggs.

They said you always deposited them

at Duckweed Swamp before."

"We thought you were tired

of the crows eating your eggs,"

said Arabella.

"So this year

you deposited the eggs

at Meadow Marsh to confuse them."

"That was my idea,"

said Mr. Turtle proudly.

"It was my idea

to stage the robbery,"

said Mrs. Turtle,

"to confuse the crows even more."

"But we figured out
who stole the eggs,"
said Arabella.
"The crows
will figure it out, too."

"Let us take the eggs

to our house," said Albert.

"The crows will never think

to look for them there."

Mr. and Mrs. Turtle

looked at each other.

"The twins are right, Mother,"

said Mr. Turtle.

"I know they are,"

said Mrs. Turtle.

"I did not know where

we could hide the eggs next."

Arabella and Albert carried the eggs

back to their house.

The kitchen light

was still on.

"Do you think Mother and Father

will be angry

because we sneaked out?"

asked Albert.

"Maybe they will be angry at first,"

said Arabella.

"But when they hear

how we found the eggs,

they will be very proud."

"I bet Grandpa

will be proudest of all!"

said Albert.

And that is exactly what happened.